To dearest Phil —
with love from Abby

The Tenth Good Thing
About Barney

The Tenth Good Thing
About Barney

Judith Viorst

Illustrated by Erik Blegvad

A TRUMPET CLUB SPECIAL EDITION

Aladdin Books
Macmillan Publishing Company
866 Third Avenue, New York, NY 10022
Collier Macmillan Canada, Inc.

First Aladdin Books edition 1975
Second Aladdin Books edition 1988

Printed in the United States of America

A hardcover edition of *The Tenth Good Thing About Barney* is available from
Atheneum Publishers, Macmillan Publishing Company.

10   9   8   7   6   5

Library of Congress Cataloging-in-Publication Data

Viorst, Judith.
The tenth good thing about Barney.

Summary: In an attempt to overcome his grief, a boy tries to think of the
ten best things about his dead cat.
[1. Death—Fiction. 2. Cats—Fiction] I. Blegvad, Erik, ill. II. Title.
III. Title: 10th good thing about Barney.
[PZ7.V816Te 1986] [E] 86-25948
ISBN 0-689-71203-0

· for Jodi Aurelio ·

The Tenth Good Thing
About Barney

My cat Barney died last Friday.
I was very sad.

I cried, and I didn't watch television.
I cried, and I didn't eat my chicken or even
the chocolate pudding.
I went to bed, and I cried.

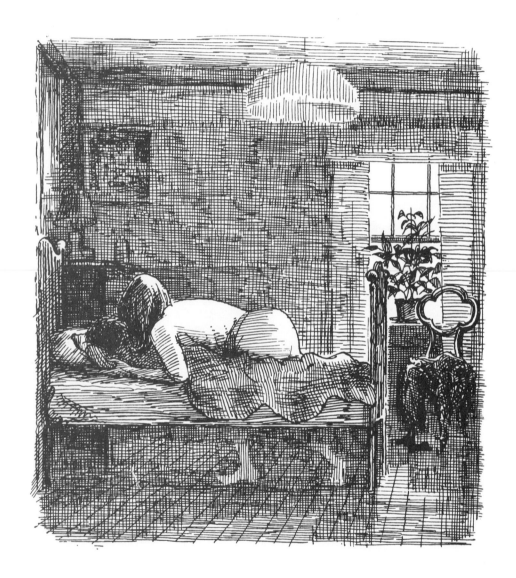

· 4 ·

My mother sat down on my bed, and she gave
me a hug.
She said we could have a funeral for Barney
in the morning.
She said I should think of ten good things
about Barney so I
could tell them at the funeral.

I thought, and I thought, and I thought of good
things about Barney.
I thought of nine good things. Then I fell
asleep.

In the morning my mother wrapped Barney in
a yellow scarf.
My father buried Barney in the ground by a
tree in the yard.
Annie, my friend from next door, came over
with flowers.
And I told good things about Barney.

Barney was brave, I said.
And smart and funny and clean.
Also cuddly and handsome, and he only once
ate a bird.
It was sweet, I said, to hear him purr in my ear.
And sometimes he slept on my belly and kept
it warm.

Those are all good things, said my mother,
but I just count nine.
I said I would try to think of another one later.

At the end of the funeral we sang a song for
Barney.

We couldn't remember any cat songs, so we
sang one about a
pussywillow.
Even my father knew the words.

Then Annie and I went into the kitchen with
Mother.
She gave us orangeade and butter cookies, and
she left the box
on the table so we could have seconds.
I gave my seconds to Annie. I miss Barney,
I said.

Annie said Barney was in heaven with lots of
cats and angels,
drinking cream and eating cans of tuna.

I said Barney was in the ground.

Heaven, said Annie, heaven. So there! The
ground, I told her,
the ground. You don't know anything.

My father came in from the yard and took a
cookie.
Big-mouthed Annie said heaven again. I said
ground.
Tell her who's right, I asked Father. She
doesn't know anything.

Maybe Barney's in heaven, my father began.
Aha, said Annie, and stuck her tongue out at
me.

And maybe, said my father, Barney isn't.
What did I tell you, I said, and yanked Annie's
braid.

Father made me let go.
We don't know too much about heaven, he
told Annie.
We can't be absolutely sure that it's there.

But if it is there, said Annie in her absolutely
sure voice,
it's bound to have room for Barney and tuna
and cream.
She finished another cookie and went back
home.

My father told me he had to work in the
garden.
I said that I would help—but only a little.
I told him I didn't like it that Barney was dead.

He said, why should I like it? It's sad, he said.
He told me that it might not feel so sad
tomorrow.

My father had a packet of little brown seeds.
He shook some out on his hand.
The ground will give them food and a place
to live, he said.
And soon they'll grow a stem and some leaves
and flowers.

I squeezed the packet open and looked down
to the bottom.
I told him, I don't see leaves and I don't see
flowers.

Things change in the ground, said my father.
In the ground everything changes.

Will Barney change too? I asked him.

Oh yes, said my father.
He'll change until he's part of the ground
in the garden.

And then, I asked, will he help to make
flowers and leaves?

He will, said my father.
He'll help grow the flowers, and he'll help
grow that tree and
some grass.
You know, he said, that's a pretty nice job
for a cat.

My father and I planted all of the seeds in
the garden.
Mother made sandwiches, and we ate them
under the tree.
After lunch we worked in the garden some
more.

At night I still didn't want to watch any
television.
When I turned out the light, my mother sat
down on my bed.
She gave me a hug, and I said I had something
to tell her.
Listen, I said, and I told the good things
about Barney.

Barney was brave, I said.
And smart and funny and clean.
Also cuddly and handsome, and he only once
ate a bird.
It was sweet, I said, to hear him purr in my ear.
And sometimes he slept on my belly and kept
it warm.

Those are all good things, said my mother,
but I still just count nine.

Yes, I said, but now I have another.

Barney is in the ground and he's helping
grow flowers.
You know, I said, that's a pretty nice job for
a cat.